The Christmas Story

with Ruth J. Morehead's Holly Babes™

A Random House PICTUREBACK®

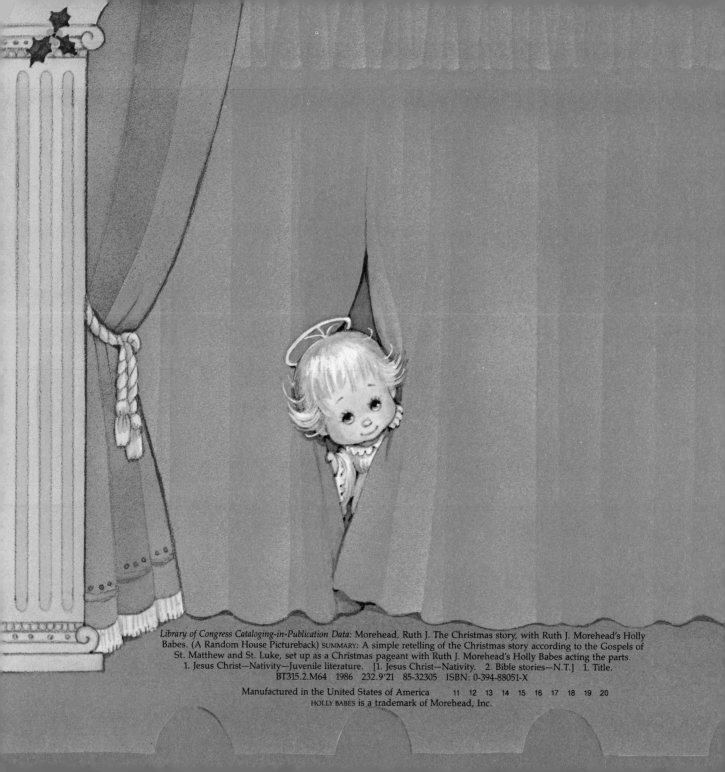

Library of Congress Cataloging-in-Publication Data: Morehead, Ruth J. The Christmas story, with Ruth J. Morehead's Holly Babes. (A Random House Pictureback) SUMMARY: A simple retelling of the Christmas story according to the Gospels of St. Matthew and St. Luke, set up as a Christmas pageant with Ruth J. Morehead's Holly Babes acting the parts. 1. Jesus Christ—Nativity—Juvenile literature. [1. Jesus Christ—Nativity. 2. Bible stories—N.T.] 1. Title. BT315.2.M64 1986 232.9′21 85-32305 ISBN: 0-394-88051-X

Manufactured in the United States of America   11   12   13   14   15   16   17   18   19   20
HOLLY BABES is a trademark of Morehead, Inc.

The Christmas Story

with Ruth J. Morehead's
Holly Babes™

Random House New York

Long, long ago a carpenter named Joseph and his wife,
Mary, lived in the city of Nazareth.

They had a small house, and they had a donkey,
but they did not have any children.

One day an angel appeared before Mary. It was the angel Gabriel.
"God has chosen you to be the mother of His son, Jesus," the
angel told Mary.

That made Mary very happy.

Not long after, Joseph and Mary had to travel to Bethlehem
to pay their taxes.
"It is a long journey," said Joseph. "But you can ride our donkey."

And so they went.

When Mary and Joseph came to Bethlehem, it was late at night
and they were very tired.

There was no room for them at the inn, but the innkeeper said they could sleep in the stable. So they went there to rest for the night.

In the stable were a cow, a lamb, a goat, and a dove.
The animals were friendly.

They let Mary use their hay for a bed.

That very night the baby was born. Mary wrapped him up
to keep him warm.

There was no crib for the baby, so Mary laid him in the animals' manger.

In the fields nearby, the shepherds who were watching
their sheep saw an angel appear in the sky.

The angel said to them, "I bring you news of great joy.
Tonight in Bethlehem, a baby has been born in a stable.
He is called Jesus Christ and he is our Lord."

The shepherds went to the stable, and when they saw the
little baby in the manger, they were filled with joy.

The shepherds knelt before little Jesus. Then they went out
to tell people what the angel had said about the newborn baby.

Far away in the east lived three wise men.

They saw a new star in the sky.

The three wise men knew the star was a sign—a sign that their Lord Jesus had been born. So the wise men set out to follow the star.

The star led them all the way to Bethlehem.

It came to rest right above a little stable.

The wise men went inside the stable. They saw
Joseph and Mary with the newborn baby.

They knelt down before the baby Jesus and gave
him gifts of gold and frankincense and myrrh.

Everyone was filled with joy. Even the animals in
the stable seemed to know how special this baby was.

Now every year at Christmas we celebrate the birth
of Jesus Christ, because he brought the good news of
God's love to the world.

The End